ALL EYES

ON OZZY!

by K-Fai Steele

Balzer + Bray
An Imprint of HarperCollins*Publishers*

Balzer + Bray is an imprint of HarperCollins Publishers.

All Eyes on Ozzy!
Copyright © 2021 by K-Fai Steele
All rights reserved. Manufactured in Italy.
No part of this book may be used or reproduced in any manner whatsoever without
written permission except in the case of brief quotations embodied in critical articles
and reviews. For information address HarperCollins Children's Books, a division of
HarperCollins Publishers, 195 Broadway, New York, NY 10007.
www.harpercollinschildrens.com

Library of Congress Control Number: 2020946927
ISBN 978-0-06-274858-4

The artist used watercolor and ink to create the illustrations for this book.
Typography by Dana Fritts
21 22 23 24 25   RTLO   10 9 8 7 6 5 4 3 2 1
❖
First Edition

For RLD, giver of attention

OZZY loved to get attention.

She always found ways to stand out,
sometimes by herself,

IN THE BIG ROCK CANNNNDY MOUNTAIN!

and sometimes with her best friends,
Zeena and Roza.

But there was one person she loved
getting attention from most of all.

Ms. Bomba was Ozzy's music teacher.
She was her *favorite* teacher.

She was *everyone's* favorite.

Ms. Bomba taught all kinds of useful stuff, like how your heartbeat will match up to the beat of a drum.

It's what makes you want to dance!

And she made learning new things fun.

One day Ms. Bomba had everyone pick
an instrument to play for the school recital:
¡Vamos a Bailar! Let's Dance!

"I'm picking the clarinet!" said Zeena.
"Dibs on the alto saxophone," said Roza.

"Rats!" thought Ozzy. "Maybe there is
a didgeridoo or a zither or a yazh." Then
she thought of the most attention-grabbing
instrument . . .

But when Ozzy got the sheet music, it wasn't so attention-grabbing after all.

"I guess I just improv the drum solo . . . ?"

"There's no drum solo in our song," said Ms. Bomba. "You play your part, and your part is to keep the beat."

Ozzy had a better idea.

For the rest of practice, Ozzy played her part.
She did it so well that Ms. Bomba gave her an
additional instrument.

Ozzy knew that everyone played their part.

Go, go, Zeena!

Take us to the bridge, Roza!

She just wished her part was better.

Ozzy didn't really see the point in playing music
if it wasn't fun, didn't make you want to dance,
and didn't match your heartbeat to the beat.

How were you supposed to feel good when
all you got was *bom-bom-bom-ding*? Ozzy
felt invisible.

The night of *¡Vamos a Bailar! Let's Dance!*
came and Ozzy was not feeling good. Her
heart was going *tumtumtumtumtumtumtum.*

"There are so many people
out there!" said Zeena.
"I can see my grandma!"
said Roza.

"I think I have to go to the
bathroom," said Ozzy. "Again."

The stage lights were hot. Ozzy was sweating.
She couldn't breathe or blink. Everyone,
including the audience, was silent.

Ms. Bomba counted the band in with her baton:
One, two, three, four!

Ozzy froze.

All around her, the trumpets, flutes, trombones, and clarinets melted into a heap of noise.

Rap! Rap! Rap! went Ms. Bomba's baton.

Ms. Bomba looked at Ozzy and
began to play the beat.

Ozzy began to tap her boot and gently hit the
drum *bom bom bom bom*.

"I think you have it now," whispered Ms. Bomba.
"Ready to lead us in?"

Ozzy held the beat for the whole band. She was
dancing and didn't even realize it.

Everyone was locked into the song, especially Ozzy.

Zeena and Roza bounced their heads. Ms. Bomba
smiled and moved her shoulders while she swung
her baton.

Afterward they all jumped up to take a bow.
Zeena and Roza squeezed Ozzy's hands and
Ozzy squeezed back and smiled at the crowd.

The applause was so loud! Her heart
went *tump tump tump tump tump.*

Now that the show was over, Ozzy
looked at Ms. Bomba for her next cue. . . .